# How Gecko Got his Knob Tail ...

Author: Pauline Cash
Illustrator: Susanna Mills

All characters appearing in this work are fictitious. Any resemblance to real persons, living or dead, is purely coincidental.



Published by Boolarong Press,
655 Toohey Road
Salisbury Qld 4107
Australia.
www.boolarongpress.com.au

First published 2015

Cataloguing-in-Publication entry available at the National Library of Australia

Creator: Cash, Pauline, author.

Title: How gecko got his knob tail... / Pauline Cash ; Susanna Mills, illustrator.

ISBN: 9781925236446 (paperback)

Target Audience: For primary school age.

Subjects: Geckos--Juvenile fiction.
Tail--Regeneration--Juvenile fiction.
Animals--Australia--Juvenile fiction.

Other Creators/Contributors: Mills, Susanna Sara, illustrator.

Dewey Number: A823.4

Printed and bound by Watson Ferguson & Company, Salisbury, Australia

Dedicated to my five children
Susan, Angela, David, Peter and Andrew

It was a hot day in Kakadu.

Gecko was half asleep by Yellow Waters.

He didn't notice hungry Crocodile swimming up quietly behind him, his big green eyes gleaming above the water.

SNAP! went Crocodile...

He bit off
Gecko's tail
and swallowed it
in one gulp!

"Ouch! Ouch!" cried Gecko.

He looked around. His tail was gone!

When they heard Gecko's cries, the other animals gathered around.

There was Possum,
piglet and Pademelon.

"Does it hurt?"

"It looks yukky".

"How will you do poos?"

"I know how to make a new tail," said Possum.

He went away and gathered some clay and herbs and berries.

Then he bandaged the mixture onto Gecko's stump.

When Gecko woke up the next morning, everything looked very strange.

He was upside down!

"Get me down! Get me down," cried Gecko.

"Don't you like your new tail?" asked Possum.

"Well, it's soft and furry," said Gecko, "but it's just not ME."

"Let me have a try," said Piglet. "I know a recipe for a tail."

So Piglet put his special mixture on Gecko's stump.

When Gecko woke up next morning he had a thin pink tail that curled round and round and round!

"It looks great," said Piglet.

"Well, it might look good to you," said Gecko, "but it's really not ME!"

While they were wondering what to do next, Brush Turkey stalked out of the rainforest.

"What is the problem?" asked Brush Turkey.
"Gecko has had his tail bitten off by a crocodile," they told him. "We're trying to give him a new one."
"I can give him a new tail," said Brush Turkey.
Can you guess what happened?

When Gecko woke up next morning, he had a beautiful feathery tail that reached up so high!

"Holy Mackerel," said Gecko, "did you think I might fly?"

"I look ridiculous and it's certainly not ME!"

"Thank you all for trying to help," said Gecko, "but my wound is healed and I want to stay just as I AM!"

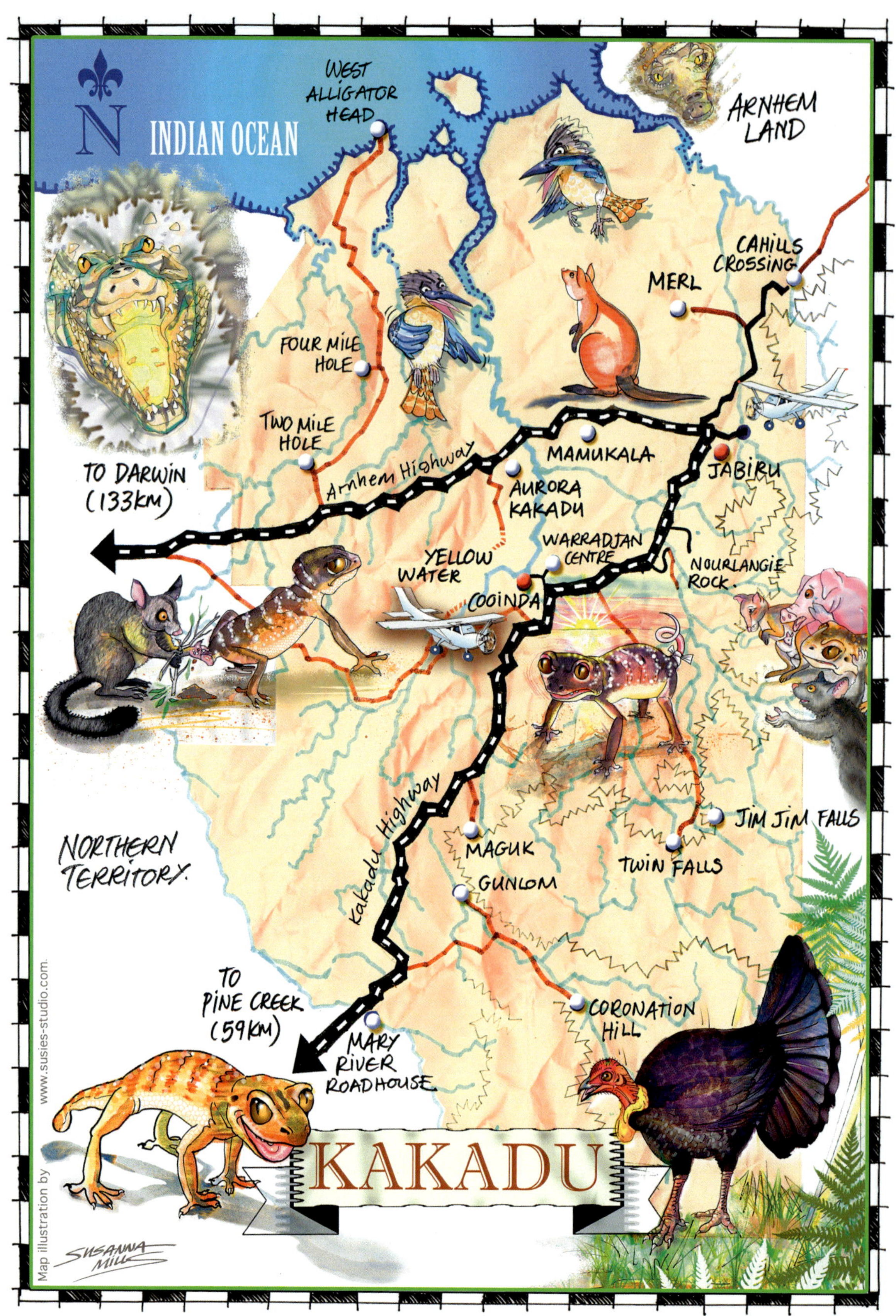
N
INDIAN OCEAN
WEST ALLIGATOR HEAD
ARNHEM LAND
CAHILLS CROSSING
MERL
FOUR MILE HOLE
TWO MILE HOLE
MAMUKALA
JABIRU
TO DARWIN (133KM)
Arnhem Highway
AURORA KAKADU
WARRADJAN CENTRE
YELLOW WATER
NOURLANGIE ROCK.
COOINDA
Kakadu Highway
JIM JIM FALLS
MAGUK
TWIN FALLS
NORTHERN TERRITORY.
GUNLOM
TO PINE CREEK (59KM)
CORONATION HILL
MARY RIVER ROADHOUSE
KAKADU
Map illustration by www.susies-studio.com.
SUSANNA MILLS

**Brush Turkey**

A large, ground-dwelling bird. Males make enormous mounds of organic matter to help hatch the female's eggs.

**Crocodile**

Kakadu is home to both saltwater and freshwater crocodiles. Be careful near any water when visiting Kakadu!

**Knob-Tailed Gecko**

A desert species from Australia. They have a broad paddle shape tail which ends in a small knob.

**Pademelon**

It looks like a small kangaroo. It is a solitary animal, found in the forests of Australia and surrounding islands.

**Piglet**

Pigs run wild in Kakadu, they eat lots of grasses, plants and beetles.

**Possum**

About the size of a domestic cat, possums live up in the trees and eat plants, insects and small animals.

**Kakadu National Park** is situated at the top of the Northern Territory, Australia. It is a World Heritage Area, listed as a UNESCO site.

Nearly 20,000 square kilometres (3.2 million acres) in size, Kakadu includes the traditional lands of many Aboriginal groups.